The Knight and the BEASTLY BATTLE

Jody Hildreth

WINDMILL BOOKS

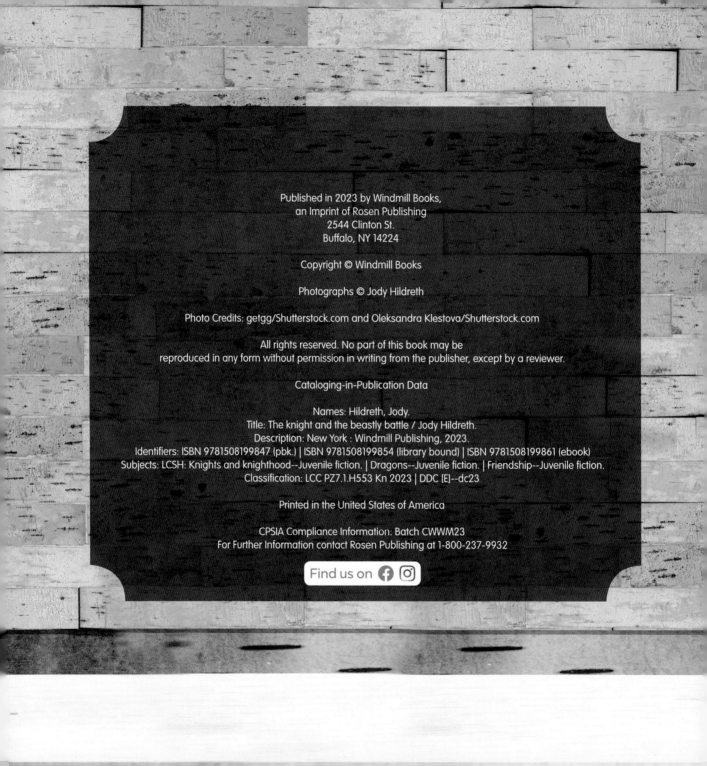

Published in 2023 by Windmill Books,
an Imprint of Rosen Publishing
2544 Clinton St.
Buffalo, NY 14224

Photographs © Jody Hildreth

Photo Credits: getgg/Shutterstock.com and Oleksandra Klestova/Shutterstock.com

Cataloging-in-Publication Data

Names: Hildreth, Jody.
Title: The knight and the beastly battle / Jody Hildreth.
Description: New York : Windmill Publishing, 2023.
Identifiers: ISBN 9781508199847 (pbk.) | ISBN 9781508199854 (library bound) | ISBN 9781508199861 (ebook)
Subjects: LCSH: Knights and knighthood--Juvenile fiction. | Dragons--Juvenile fiction. | Friendship--Juvenile fiction.
Classification: LCC PZ7.1.H553 Kn 2023 | DDC [E]--dc23

Printed in the United States of America

CPSIA Compliance Information: Batch CWWM23
For Further Information contact Rosen Publishing at 1-800-237-9932

Find us on

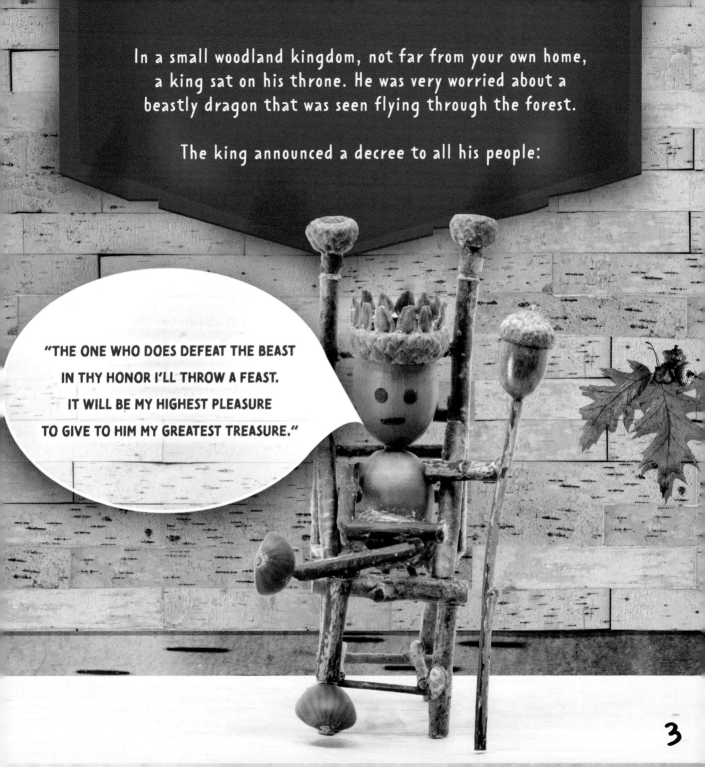

In a small woodland kingdom, not far from your own home, a king sat on his throne. He was very worried about a beastly dragon that was seen flying through the forest.

The king announced a decree to all his people:

"THE ONE WHO DOES DEFEAT THE BEAST IN THY HONOR I'LL THROW A FEAST. IT WILL BE MY HIGHEST PLEASURE TO GIVE TO HIM MY GREATEST TREASURE."

3

All who heard the king's message were very excited, but few had the courage to stand up to such a terrible beast. But there was one who had courage beyond others: Sir Crackemup. He vowed to defeat this terrible beast.

Sir Crackemup thought of the king's promise of precious treasure. What could it be? Gold? Diamonds? Maybe even the hand of his beautiful daughter, Princess Nutmeg? Whatever it was, surely the brave knight would come out victorious.

Sir Crackemup spent two days tracking the beast through the woods. He found footprints, claw marks on trees, and even small burned branches. Late one afternoon, he caught his first glimpse of the giant creature, and even though he was filled with courage, his legs began to shake like a willow in the wind.

The knight wasted no time and decided to attack right away. With sword drawn and shield held in front, he charged directly at the dragon. The dragon stopped the knight's charge with a ferocious blast of fiery flames.

Sir Crackemup was smoking mad. He had made a big mistake by not planning his attack. He took time to fix his burned armor, then began to plot his next attack.

Sir Crackemup knew he was not fast enough to attack the dragon on his own, so he decided to use his trusty steed, Cinnamon. He also trained for many hours using a lance. This spear was much longer than his sword. Surely now he would be able to take down the mighty beast and earn the king's treasure.

Sir Crackemup and Cinnamon discovered
the beast resting in a mossy log. With
thundering hoofbeats, they made a swift
attack on the dragon, who woke quickly and
faced the deadly sharpness of the lance.

Unfortunately, Cinnamon did not have as much courage as Sir Crackemup.

With two losses in battle, Sir Crackemup decided even
more planning was needed. He spied on the beast, trying
to find some weakness. He discoverd that the beast loved
the dragon berries which were just beginning to ripen.
This gave the knight an idea. Perhaps a clever mind would
defeat this dragon rather than strength.

Sir Crakemup sheathed his sword and strapped on a large basket. He harvested as many dragon berries as he could and carried the berries deep into the woods near a spot where the dragon loved to take naps.

He created a tasty trail of berries leading to a large pit he dug in the ground. However, he was so excited about his clever plan that he didn't sense the danger sneaking up behind him.

He barely escaped, with only his buns slightly toasted. Sir Crackemup decided to take some more time to plan his next attack. After all, the seasons were changing from fall to winter, and surely the dragon would be hibernating in some remote place when the air turned cold.

One wintry day, a young lad name Huck was out exploring in the woods. He had dreams of becoming a brave knight, like his hero Sir Crackemup. However, his parents would not let Huck play with anything sharp. While walking through fields of white snow, something red caught his eye. It was the feathers of an arrow. Bright red - just like the ones used by Sir Crackemup.

Maybe he could return the arrow and get to meet his hero. He bent down to pull the arrow from the frozen ground, but it was really stuck. As he pulled harder, it felt as though the earth began to shake. One final tug and the arrow came free, but a low grumble suddenly rattled in his ears. Was it an earthquake?

The arrow wasn't stuck in the ground, but rather in the rump of the beast! Huck became as frozen as the forest around him when the dragon rose and faced him. Surely he would be eaten! But instead, the dragon threw the young boy onto his neck, overjoyed at having that painful stick pulled from his backside. In that moment, the boy knew this would be the start of a very unique friendship, one that would prove to be more valuable than any precious treasure the king could have offered.